RAPTURE:
The Big Daddy

"I chose… Rapture!"

Andrew Ryan's piped-in speech came to its climax just as the underwater city appeared before the window of our bathysphere.

Little Maddie's mouth dropped open at the sight of the bright neon signs, imposing statues, and looming buildings that slowly revealed themselves amidst the deep blue water. I picked her up and propped her on my hip so she could get a better look. Her small fingers splayed against the glass bubble of the watercraft as her wide blue eyes roamed the scenery.

I cast a glance at Clara. She looked equally as entranced, despite the arms crossed over her chest. Despite the skeptical look on her face. But in her eyes, there was wonder. And fascination.

A small smile curved my mouth. Months of talking, months of persuading… Convincing my wife of just under five years to leave our quaint little hometown in Ohio behind, of uprooting our daughter just as she was about to start school, so we could start over in the near-mythical capitalist's dream, also known as Rapture, had been difficult, to say the least. But I knew it was the right choice.

"So, as I was saying, Mr. Winters," Sean Rigby -- our realtor, and the spindly man who'd glued himself to the back of the bathysphere during the whole descent -- said, clearing his throat. Ryan's speech continued to stream through the speakers, but his words went unheard as Rigby resumed his shtick. "Apollo Square is a very family-friendly area with lots of facilities I'm sure you'll find to your liking. It's close to Fontaine's Department Store, and the Ryan the Lion Preparatory Academy is just a few connective tubes away." His attention drifted to Maddie. "Your little one's about the age to go to school, right? Have you given any thought to picking a school yet?"

I shook my head Detailed information about Rapture had been hard to come by back in the States. Or, on the surface, rather. We were going into this a little blind, and that's probably what scared Clara. "Not yet."

"What's this? Ryan the Lion?" she asked, raising an eyebrow as she tore her gaze from the watery metropolis. She smirked at me. "Sounds like someone's got an ego."

"Well, I think you'll find that it's a well deserved one, ma'am," Rigby said, then dipped his head apologetically. "Begging your pardon."

"You'd have to have an ego to build a place like this," I found myself saying as I turned my attention back to the city. Maddie was leaning forward now, her face so close to the glass that her breath was leaving a circle of fog on it.

"Wow," she breathed, her mouth stuck in a permanent smile ever since we'd begun our descent. "Is this real, Daddy? Really real?" She twisted around to look at me, and I nodded. She giggled and leaned back into me, her arms wrapping around my neck. "Are we really gonna live under the water?"

"We sure are, pumpkin."

She gasped and marveled at a whale that glided by as our bathysphere drew nearer to the city. I tried to read each and every one of those neon signs, but it was too much to take in all at once. A pink and

3

yellow sign that read *Cohen's Collection: Fine Arts*. A green theatre marquis: *Fleet Hall*. A circular sign: *Bella Mia's High Fashion*. Now at least I know where Clara will be spending all her time... There was a sign for a casino called *Sir Prize*, and another that caught my interest: *Robertson's Tobaccoria*. Good. I'd been under the impression I'd have to quit. And so had Clara.

We soon dipped into a circular tunnel, whose supports were crowned with a series of signs that lit up as we neared them. I read each as we passed.

All Good Things...

Of This Earth...

Flow...

Into The City

A touch too idealistic for my tastes, but a little optimism never hurt anyone. If this place was even half what people had made it out to be, it'd be good enough for me.

The bathysphere slowed as we approached a chamber and gradually came to a stop. There was the whir of machinery from somewhere behind us, the sound of water draining, and a moment later, the door of the vessel slid open.

"And here we are," Rigby said as I let Maddie down. "The Apollo Square." He took a few steps past us, out onto the long hallway that the door had opened to. "Now, the great thing about the Artemis Suites is that it's literally less than a minute away." He motioned for us to follow him out. I grabbed Maddie's hand and began reaching for one of our suitcases when he shook his head. "No, no. I'll have someone bring your things shortly. For now, how about I show you your new home?"

"That sounds nice," Clara said with a sigh.

So I left our bags, took Clara's hand with my free one, and followed Rigby down the glass-roofed corridor, up a flight of stairs, and into a tall building labeled *Artemis Suites*.

Apollo Square was a working class neighborhood, Rigby had explained during the short walk there. The name Artemis Suites was a misnomer. The units were humble abodes, which Clara and I had already resigned ourselves to. But, with a bit a luck, and a lot of sweat and hard work, I was sure we'd be up in Olympus Heights soon enough. Andrew Ryan's philosophy all but guaranteed it.

Our fourth floor apartment was small, but had two bedrooms, a kitchen, a bathroom, and a living room. All came furnished, which was business as usual here. There weren't many people looking to -- or who could even afford to -- ship all their furniture all the way down here.

There wasn't a window to be found in any of these rooms, which made sense, but was also a bit of a disappointment. Maddie would've loved to be able to watch fish and whales outside her bedroom window. No, Rapture seemed pretty paranoid about water leaks -- and with good reason. Amongst the plethora of posters plastered in the hallway where we'd left the bathysphere, there had been at least half a dozen demanding people to contact the authorities if they so much as felt a drop of water hit them.

"And if you decide to paint or put up wallpaper, don't forget to turn on the ventilation accelerator," Rigby reminded as he showed us the switch in the kitchen. "Wouldn't want you folks passing out from the fumes, now."

After showing us around our new place, and the building at large, Clara and I signed the necessary papers to make everything official. He offered a tour of Rapture itself, but we declined. Clara was obviously tired, and I thought it'd be more interesting to explore the city on our own.

"Well, I suppose that's it for now, then," Rigby said at the front door as he handed over a set of keys for its lock. "I think you'll find tomorrow to be another exciting day, Mr. Winters," he said as I took the ring of keys. "There are a number of prime locations that Ryan Industries is currently looking to lease. I'm sure we'll find the perfect spot for your timepiece shop."

I nodded, pocketing the keys. "Let's hope so."

He smiled and gave a jovial laugh. "I'll see you then. Sir, ma'am." He dipped his head to each of us in turn. "Little one." He patted Maddie on the head.

"Bye-bye!" she called after him, waving enthusiastically as he left down the hall.

Clara urged her inside, and I closed the door, testing out the keys to make sure they worked. Once satisfied, I joined them in the kitchen.

"Look. A housewarming gift," Clara said with a wry smile as she held up a handful of papers. Flyers similar to the ones posted on the walls. They advertised everything from doctor's clinics, to department stores, and even a police station.

"Where'd you find those?" I asked as I took one. *The Little Sister's Orphanage* it read. I didn't expect that kind of charity in a place like this.

"The drawer by the stove." She leafed through the rest. "Now, what on earth is a Plasmid?"

"Who knows? Maybe one day we'll find out." I left the flyer on the counter and looked to Maddie, who was fascinated enough with the diamond pattern on the linoleum. "Well, this is it," I said, bringing my gaze back to my wife. "There's no going back now."

She smiled back. "Good. I've got a good feeling about this place."

***

I got up early the next morning to meet with Rigby. The sooner I found a place for my shop, the sooner I could get to work and become part of this Great Chain.

Sleep had been hard to come by last night. Partly because of the excitement of the move, and partly because Maddie slept between Clara and I -- and she flails more than a fish out of water. The bed we'd found in her room was actually a crib, so the arrangement was a temporary measure until we could find something more suitable for a four-year-old.

The girls and I had breakfast at Finley's Eat-In Take-Out, which was located in the aptly named Welcome Center. From there, I left to find Rigby, but only after Clara assured me she'd be able to find her way back to Apollo Square on her own. I had a feeling she wanted to hit up a few stores of her own liking along the way.

While Artemis Suites admittedly had a claustrophobic feel to it, the boardwalks of Rapture were more spacious and open-aired than I'd imagined. Here, the use of windows was fearless. Large walls of reinforced glass extended up even into the ceiling. The water outside was a little green, a little murky, but still beautiful nevertheless. Schools of fish swam by every so often, and there were eels and manta rays and even a few sharks. Just the thought of having a shop that faced a view like that... It was great.

I met Rigby on Market Street. The hub of everyday life at Rapture, he'd said. Full of businesses of every size and shape, from bars to shoeshine stands.

"To be honest, I don't think we have any timepiece shops down here," he said as we made our way along the boulevard. "I'm sure the department stores sell watches and clocks, of course, but I don't think we've got a specialty shop like you're talking about starting."

"Glad to hear it." A timepiece shop had been my dream since I was just a kid. Since I apprenticed under Cleveland's premier clockmaker. After years of assisting, giving up my afternoons and weekends to learn and perfect the craft, the old man ended up leaving the shop to his daughter, who promptly sold it to a competing larger chain. My career had taken a different turn after that. I'd worked various jobs trying to save up to open a shop of my own, but there wasn't enough demand for another one. So I saved and saved, and then I met Clara, and then we both saved. And then I heard whispers about Rapture.

The capitalist's wet dream. A true laissez-faire economy. No regulations or laws to damper the free market. Andrew Ryan, the creator of Rapture and founder of Ryan Industries, had put it much more eloquently in his speech that played in the bathysphere yesterday.

Rigby showed me several available spaces along Market Street. None of them seem badly placed as far as foot traffic was concerned, so I would've been happy with anything, so long as it was in my price range.

After a few hours, I settled on a small but comfortable space in the upper area, nestled between a kiosk for the Rapture Tribune and a place called Sinclair Spirits. The rent was just under the limit of what I could afford.

A rush of excitement passed through me as I signed the lease papers and counted out the down payment, but I knew it was still too early to celebrate. There was still the matter of sourcing the materials to even make the damn clocks. I'd brought some of my finest work down with me, either as samples, or to sell, but I'd have to start crafting them down here soon enough. Acquiring wood, glass, metal, and quartz would be a much harder task here than back on the surface. But it was a challenge I was prepared for.

That afternoon, I showed Clara and Maddie the space, and belatedly got their approval. We found another restaurant for lunch over on High Street -- which was certainly called so for a reason. Rigby said that was where the Rapture elite shopped, and the prices reflected that. One day, I hoped, the three of us would be walking that boulevard regularly.

The next few days passed in a blur. I looked into finding companies to source materials for my business and worked on the legalities of even opening the shop while Clara looked into schools for Maddie and prowled the Farmer's Market, hoping to adapt our diet into something that still halfway resembled what it had been back on the surface.

Rapture had no cows. That probably seemed like an obvious thing, but with no grassy pastures, most of the usual farm animals were missing here. I'd heard Fontaine Farms had chickens and a breed of small pigs, but that was about it. The market was full of fish, fruits and vegetables grown using hydroponics, and once exotic but now common foods like sea urchin and lamprey.

By the end of the week, Clara had most of our apartment furnished according to her tastes, and Maddie had a big girl's bed. On Saturday, we had our first sit-down dinner. Clara was practically glowing at the opportunity to finally use the kitchen for something more substantial than snacks and hurried breakfasts.

"It's been so difficult getting her on a proper nap schedule here," Clara said, shooting Maddie a look as we ate at the table that evening. "I guess it's the lack of sunlight here. I hadn't really thought about that before." She delicately cut into her chicken breast while Maddie carefully separated her peas from her carrots. "Won't that mess with our circadian rhythms or something?"

"I think it'll just take a while to get used to," I replied with a nod. I'd been having the same trouble with sleep lately. "The lights around here run on a schedule. So it shouldn't be too hard."

Clara's blue eyes narrowed a little at my answer. She was obviously disappointed. "I never really thought about it before. I just assumed we'd still be able to see the sun."

"Once we move to Olympus Heights, we'll have all the sunlight we need." I smiled at the thought.

Maddie's spoonful of vegetables paused halfway to her mouth as her eyes grew wide. She had inherited everything from her mother when it came to her looks. The same fiery red hair, the light blue eyes, the pale complexion. And every bit as beautiful. "Olympus Heights? What's that? When're we moving?"

"In maybe five years, with any luck," I said, picking up a pea that fell off her spoon.

Clara raised her brow. "Luck? I thought Rapture was all about hard work."

I grinned back at her, shaking my head, and took a drink of my champagne. Our first purchase from Sinclair Spirits. It would take some getting used to, but it wasn't as big of a change as that synthetic tobacco that Robertson's sold. Forget sunlight -- if anything it was *that* stuff that needed some getting used to. I'd have to ask around and see if there was anyone that sold the real stuff.

Over the next several days, I worked on my shop. Got the permits and license, started ordering the signage, and secured enough materials to make more timepieces to fill my display window.

11

When I asked my girls what I should call the shop, Maddie's reply had been both enthusiastic and immediate.

"Ticks!" she said with a smile.

***

Two weeks later, Ticks was open for business. It was a one-man operation, but I wasn't looking to hire any assistants just yet. Business was slow starting off, and I took a neighboring shopkeeper's advice and bought an ad for the place with Rapture Radio. Within just a few days of the ad airing, the foot traffic at Ticks picked up. With the orders coming in, and the supplies located, I finally dove back into my passion: making clocks.

After careful consideration, Clara and I decided that, despite its name, Ryan the Lion Preparatory Academy would be the best fit for Maddie. She had to take several tests, but ultimately, she was accepted, and the staff there ensured us she'd be given the best education Rapture had to offer. This was a bold claim, considering how many schools there were here. But Ryan the Lion seemed like the cream of the crop when it came to our budget.

That was another thing Clara didn't like about this place at first, but I assured her it was better this way. Free schooling was something people took for granted back on the surface, but I was willing to shell out to give my little girl the tools she needed to lead a successful life. And Clara couldn't argue with that.

Maddie seemed to be enjoying the school well enough. She was a naturally social kid, always eager to make new friends and discover new things. She'd already gotten close with a couple other kids at Artemis Suites.

Clara had also made friends of her own. Not just here in Apollo Square, but also amongst the women that frequented Market Street. Using her natural charm, she even managed to drum up some business for me. Maybe I'd have to put her on my payroll after all.

***

The bell dangling from the front door of Ticks chimed softly, indicating a new customer. I put down the escapement wheel and file I'd been working with and stood up from my stool behind the counter to greet them.

It was a man about my age. Early thirties. Skinny. A little sloppy. He doffed his hat to me as he noticed my attention, revealing a head of greased brown hair.

"Well good morning there, sir," he said with a grin. His attention strayed over my clocks in the display window as he made his way over to my counter. "Nice place ya got here. I knew someone'd gobble up this little piece of real estate in a Rapture minute." He extended his hand to me. "Lionel Groose. Pleased to meet ya."

I shook his hand. "Arthur Winters. The pleasure's all mine."

Lionel chuckled, taking a step back to survey the line of clocks set up in the glass case at the

13

counter. "Welcome to Rapture. How ya liking it so far?"

"Quite a lot, if I don't say so myself," I replied. I was about to ask how he knew I was new, but in a place like this, I'm sure immigrants were few, and word traveled fast. "Thanks for stopping by, Lionel." I came around the end of the counter to join him, hoping he was here for more than just introductions. "Are you looking for anything in particular?"

The man nodded vaguely as his half-lidded eyes settled on the clocks. "I was wondering if you had any of those skeleton clocks. You know, with the exposed cogs and all that."

"Not at the moment. I didn't bring much of my stock with me, so what you see here is about all I have right now," I admitted. "But a skeleton clock, you say? I can have one for you in about a week."

"Ah." The man's face brightened. "So you takin' special orders and whatnot? I might like to pick out the details."

"Of course." I pulled my pen and pad of paper from the pocket of my shirt. "What did you have in mind?"

"Well, maybe I shoulda brought the lady down here," he said with a sheepish laugh. "She's got quite a particular taste, that one does."

"Is it a gift for her?"

"Sure is."

"Bring her down anytime and we'll work something out," I said, tucking the pen and paper away for now. "But if you're sure it's a skeleton clock you want, I can go ahead and get started with the basics."

"That'd be great."

"Are you looking for a wall clock, a wrist watch -- "

"Something like this," he said, pointing to a mantle clock finished with oak and brass. "About that size and shape."

"That I can do."

"So." His hands slid into the pockets of his slacks as he continued to peruse my display. "Where are you from?"

"Ohio," I replied. "Cleveland, to be specific."

"Ah. That's the one near Lake Erie, right?"

"You got it."

"Nice. Never been, but it sounds nice. Anything by a lake's nice, right?" He looked serious, but then a smile spread over his lips. As if he just realized the humor in what he'd said. "Look at where I'm sayin' this. We're in the frickin' middle of the ocean right now. Sometimes I forget..."

I couldn't imagine that being hard to forget, but maybe after a while, it was possible.

"So where are you from?" I asked.

"Pontus Flats, over on the south end of Apollo Square," he said. For a moment, he left it at that, but it was quickly followed with a laugh. "No, I know what you mean. Jefferson City. Jefferson City, Missouri."

"Yeah? How long have you been down here?"

"Oh, it's been about five years now," he said, absently scratching at the patchy stubble on his chin. "Came down with dreams of owning my own business and becoming the next Andrew Ryan, but I'm working over at Fontaine's Department Store now. Bathysphere DeLuxe, actually. Turns out I'm pretty handy myself when it comes to fixing things."

I simply nodded at that. I was curious about why things didn't seem to have worked out for him, but I didn't want to pry. And I didn't want it to deter me from my own dream.

"So in other words, if you're ever in the market for a private bathysphere, I'm your guy," he said, indicating himself with his thumb. "I know my way around one of those better than a woman these days. Anyway, speaking of women, I'll try bringing my lady around this weekend. You'll be open then, right?"

I nodded. "Open every day of the week." Down here, religion and church were long forgotten. Just about every establishment was open on Sundays. "I'll have some sketches ready for you then."

"Thanks. Looking forward to it," he said, shaking my hand again. He pulled his hat back on as he headed for the door. "It's been nice makin' your acquaintance."

"Same here." I smiled as he left. The bell signaled his exit. Through the shop windows I watched him walk down the boulevard for a moment before returning to my workbench behind the counter.

My first custom order.

***

That Sunday, Lionel did in fact return to my shop with his wife. We talked for about an hour and designed the clock of her dreams. I used the sizeable deposit to treat Clara and I to a nice dinner and a show at one of Sander Cohen's shows. It was our sixth wedding anniversary. I bought her that latest record from Grace Holloway, an up-and-coming jazz singer whom she fawned over, and she almost wanted to skip the play and go straight home to give it a listen.

We left Maddie with a friend of Clara's at Artemis Suites -- a fellow mother, whose child was friends with Maddie. To be honest, she probably didn't even notice we were gone. Too wrapped up in watching her favorite new cartoon: *Ryan the Lion and Peter the Parasite*.

Clara was dressed to the nines, donning a new dress from that high fashion place up in High Street. She looked like a million bucks in that green strapless gown.

Not wanting me to drag her down -- or at least, that's how it seemed from my view of things -- she bought me a new suit, which was by far the most expensive thing I'd worn since our wedding. And even that tux had been just a rental.

We took our seats in the audience as the lights dimmed around us. Clara flipped through her bulletin. The name of the musical was *Patrick and Moira*. Her friends had recommended it to her as a must-see, so here we were.

"I hear his name all over the place. Apparently he's quite the artistic genius here in Rapture," she said quietly as I settled beside her.

"Hm? Who's that?"

"Sander Cohen." She indicated his name in big letters on the playbill. "Sculptor, poet, composer, playwright. Seems like he does a little bit of everything around here."

"Cohen? I think I've heard that name before," I said, remembering as spotlights hit the stage. "Didn't he write Rapture's anthem?"

Clara nodded. "'Rise, Rapture, Rise,' if I'm not mistaken."

If there was anything that could be said for the people that comprised this place known as Rapture, it was that they were far from humble. It was almost refreshing to see such unbridled confidence. Here, there was no one to shame you into stepping back into line, to holding back and being average. It was a place where everyone was free to excel however they liked. And if that meant a guy with a face caked up with exaggerated makeup wanted to crash the stage in the middle of his own play and usurp the lead female's role... who was I to judge?

Besides, the play was a little weird even before that.

***

Before I knew it, three years had gone by. Raced by, it seemed. And in that time, my shop grew. We relocated to High Street. Now, I had four employees on my payroll, and it felt like we hardly ever closed. Everyone in Rapture knew Ticks, and everyone knew the quality watches and clocks we produced here.

We'd moved from Apollo Square to Olympus Heights, although the lower-end section of the district. Now, we called Athena's Glory home. It was a far cry from Artemis Suites. Maddie loved it all the same. Clara, more so.

18

Our little girl was doing great at Ryan the Lion. Top of her class, two years running. We started getting solicitations from other schools, all vying to have her as a student. Schools were competitive down here, all in search of the brightest students, all hoping to churn out as many future innovators as possible. Maddie was everyone's idea of the perfect daughter. I could only imagine how difficult keeping the boys away from her would be in another five years.

I headed home from another long but productive day at work as the lights of the boardwalk on High Street dimmed, signaling the beginning of the evening hours. When I reached our apartment, I found it empty. The lights were off. I flicked them on and found a note on the kitchen counter.

Hi Honey,

I'm taking Madeline out for some shopping at Fontaine's. We should be back not long after you get home from work. I've got something special for dinner planned, so don't ruin your appetite!

Love,

Clara

I smiled as I read over it again, then undid the first few buttons of my shirt and opened the collar a little before sinking into my brown recliner. I grabbed the TV remote from the coffee table and settled in for the latest edition of Rapture Reports.

An hour went by, and then two. The news was over and a documentary about the life of Andrew Ryan was playing.

A third hour passed. It was nearing nine o'clock. By then, I'd already left Athena's Glory and grabbed the first train headed for Fontaine's Department Store. It was unusual for Clara to be late. For anything. Maybe she and Maddie had just lost track of time -- that store was practically a whole world in itself. But something about it didn't sit right with me.

I was still trying to decide which department to check first as I entered the building. Just about each one seemed viable, so I had quite the task ahead of me.

I approached the clerk at the front desk of the lobby to ask if she'd seen Clara and Maddie around. Rapture was still only just a city, and not a very big one when it came to population, so it was easy to remember people. Before the question could leave my mouth, I heard a familiar voice. Clara's.

"No, please! Can't you just -- Until we find her," she said, sobbing through her hands. She was standing a ways over on the other side of the lobby. A security guard stood before her. "She can't have gone far."

"Ma'am," the security guard said with a sigh, "we can't close down the entire building for one lost little girl."

Before I knew what I was doing, I had shouldered past a crowd of people who'd gathered around.

"Clara? What's wrong? Where's Maddie?" I asked, noticing she wasn't anywhere in sight.

Clara's eyes were red. Her mascara had smeared and trailed down her cheeks. "Oh, Arthur! She's gone! I can't find her anywhere. I looked and looked -- " Her words were cut short when she grasped my shoulders and buried her face in my chest.

My heart raced hard at the thought, but I tried to keep calm. Maddie usually wasn't one to wander. How could this happen?

"Where? Have you looked everywhere? Where did you last see her?" I asked frantically. "How long ago was this?"

"Almost two hours," she choked out. "We were in the bookstore up on the third floor. She asked if she could look at the books in the children's aisle. I said yes, but when I came to check on her a few minutes later, she was gone."

"Sir, we're currently in the midst of searching building top to bottom," the security guard said, looking annoyed. "If your little girl's here, we'll find her. This is a big place. Chances are she's just playing hide-and-seek, like kids do. Wouldn't be the first time it's happened."

His words were meant to be reassuring, but they only made me more anxious. Maddie wasn't the type of girl to play that kind of joke. She didn't enjoy tricking adults like some kids did. It just wasn't in her nature.

But still, I hoped. Hoped this was the one time that she was that type of girl. Because if this wasn't a joke, if she's wasn't just playing around, then that meant... No, I couldn't even think about it. I shook my head of the thought.

"We'll find her. It'll be okay," I said to Clara, embracing her tightly.

"I can't believe it. We were only separated for a few minutes," she whispered, as if cursing herself.

"You stay here in the lobby just in case she finds her way here." I pulled away, wiping her tears. "I'll go help the guards look."

Clara just nodded as she pulled a tissue from her purse. I left her there, found the nearest elevator, and took it up to the third floor.

My appearance must've mirrored my frame of mind, because I got several strange looks from customers as the doors dinged open and I rushed past them. The bookstore was nearby. I made a straight line for it.

There was a trio of security guards standing near a stairway leading up, chatting in a half-circle. I swallowed down my irritation and ignored them.

Frantically, calling Maddie's name all the way, I searched the entire bookstore. So much so that the clerk behind the counter kept trying to get me to leave.

"Oh jeez, not again! Wherever she is, she's not here," the older woman had said while waving me off dismissively.

I stayed until I had covered the whole place. Sure enough, there was no sign of Maddie. I paced the concourse, eyes sweeping left and right, searching for any hint of a clue. In the end, I came up with nothing. After going through the neighboring departments, I drew too much attention, and two of the guards led me back down to the lobby. My heart sank when I saw Clara still standing there, alone.

The official search of the building ended a half hour later. By then, I had already searched the nearby connective tunnel, bathysphere port, and train station. Not only was there no sign of Maddie, no one I asked even remembered seeing her come through.

Clara and I were sent on our way shortly after. As she collected herself, I asked the woman at the front desk to put in a call through to the cops.

The woman just stared at me and asked, "Which one?"

***

We ended up at the nearest police station: Poppadopolis Police Department. One of almost a dozen different outfits in Rapture, I soon learned. Down here, there was no ubiquitous 911 to call. Even emergency services and criminal cases were handled by private entities.

"Look, Mr. Winters, she's only been gone for a few hours," the officer sitting a desk apart from me said, pen twirling between his fingers. "Our rules down here are much the same as back on the surface. Missing isn't missing until twenty-four hours have passed."

"Twenty-four hours?" I almost shouted. "She's seven! She can't be away from home that long."

He just shrugged. His expression remained the same: blank. "You know, despite all the hoopla, Rapture isn't that big of a place. She can't have gone far. I'm sure she'll be home tomorrow -- "

"Not if no one's looking for her!"

" -- by her own volition, I was going to say," he ground out, looking irritated at my interruption. "If she's lost, I'm sure she knows to ask for help, right?"

I couldn't believe what I was hearing. "What do you mean *if* she's lost? Of course she's lost. Either that, or..." The words just wouldn't form. "Wherever she is right now, she's in danger."

Another twenty minutes in that synthetic tobacco-filled office with Detective Ambrose didn't get me anywhere. He obviously didn't care. Wouldn't care until twenty-four hours had passed. I broke the news to Clara, who was waiting in the lobby.

"Then let's just try a different station," she said. "I heard the McMurray Police Station is almost as highly praised as Poppadopolis."

I shook my head. I'd asked Ambrose about that. He'd said the twenty-four hour rule was the industry-wide standard in Rapture.

"Why don't you go on home?" I said tiredly, happening to glance at the time on my wristwatch. It was already almost midnight. "Who knows? Maybe Maddie will be there, waiting. Maybe she somehow got lost and just headed home."

From the look on her face, I could tell Clara didn't want to, but instead of saying anything, she just broke down again.

"I'll keep looking. I'll call if I find anything new."

***

I spent literally the whole night looking. And I came up with nothing. No stray shoe, no familiar hair ribbon, and no witnesses who said they'd seen Maddie at all yesterday. By the time I trudged home, the morning lights were on, and my shop was the one desolate dark spot on the High Street boardwalk. I couldn't even bear to think of opening it now. I'd have to call my employees when I got home and tell them not to bother coming in.

Clara and I couldn't stand to wait the full twenty-four hours, so just before noon, we found ourselves again seated in the lobby of Poppadopolis Police Department.

Detective Ambrose didn't look any happier to see us today, but he waved us into his office without comment as he puffed away on his cigarette.

"I was sure she'd have shown up by now. They usually do," he said by way of greeting as he gestured for us to take the chairs before his desk. He sat down in his own chair and began rummaging through a drawer. "So, I suppose we should get the fee figured out first..."

Clara sniffed into her tear-soaked tissue as she peered up at him with tired eyes. "Fee?"

Ambrose simply nodded as he shuffled through the papers he'd pulled from his desk. "We have several different packages for these types of cases. Take a look through these, and -- "

"Packages?" I sat straighter in my chair. "What the hell are you talking about? Why can't you just send out officers to start looking?"

He blinked at me, as if I'd just said something ridiculous. "Well, yes, Mr. Winters, that is what we'll be doing, but only once you've chosen your service package. You'll see here that with our platinum package, we can have up to five officers out within twenty-four hours. However, as we're bogged down

25

with other cases at the moment, the price is a little steeper than usual." He indicated a paper he slid before Clara and me as he talked. "And here we have the gold package, which is probably more your style. With it, we can have up to three officers out by the end of the week. I think you'll find the price manageable."

"You're kidding..." Those were the only words that left my mouth as I scanned over the documents. Packages. Like he was selling insurance. Theft, robbery, kidnapping, rape, murder. All covered in these various packages, with the promise of dedicated man-hours to resolve them for a certain amount of money.

"You're welcome to shop around, but I think you'll find our prices more than competitive," he added with a smile, proud.

"Wait. What does this mean?" Clara asked, giving me a wary look.

"It means we have to pay them if we want them to find Maddie," I said, the words weighing heavy on my tongue.

Ambrose cleared his throat. "To *look* for her, that is. We make no guarantees we can find any missing persons."

"How much?" I asked.

"For which package?"

"The best you've got. Platinum, or whatever."

"Platinum runs at a flat fee of $10,000," he replied, taking a puff on his cigarette. "As I said, at least five officers out within twenty-four hours, and we promise a minimum of one thousand hours' investigation time."

"Honey, can we afford something like that?" Clara asked me.

"Yes, we can." It would be almost all of our savings, but it was worth it. Anything was worth it. I squeezed her hand before returning my attention to Ambrose. "Then what about until then? Until the officers are deployed tomorrow?"

The man shrugged. "To be honest, we're quite swamped right now. If I had the extra men to put on this case, I'd assign them in a heartbeat, for a small additional fee. But we simply don't have the manpower."

***

Clara and I left the station ten grand poorer and no less worried.

"I'm going to keep looking," I told her as we reached the train station. I couldn't go home yet. Not without Maddie.

We parted ways there. Clara said she'd check with Maddie's teachers and classmates to see if she could get any info. I headed back to Fontaine's Department Store to look for clues. Hours later, I left with nothing. Too discouraged to return to Athena's Glory, I instead headed to Ticks. I opened the front door, but left all the lights off and didn't set out any of my wares. I wasn't here to sell.

All I could think about was how I'd last seen Maddie. She'd seen me off to work with a kiss in the morning. Said goodbye as I headed out the front door. She was so excited for a presentation she was going to give in her class. She'd spent the night before reciting it forwards and back. The thought of never seeing her precious face again... My body shook at the notion. A tumult of emotions I didn't have the strength to face.

For what seemed like hours, I just sat at the stool behind my counter in darkness, deep in thought. Perhaps I should be with Clara right now, but I couldn't bear the thought. I couldn't go back without our little girl.

My thoughts were disrupted as I heard the bell above my front door ring. Damn. I'd forgotten to lock it after I'd come in. I started to tell whoever it was to go away before I even raised my head.

It was Lionel.

He gave me a wary look, stepping slowly in the shop.

"What's going on here, Arthur? Lose at the slots down at Sir Prize again?" he asked, a forced smile on his face.

I just shook my head. I didn't have the heart to tell him to get lost, though I should've. "Sorry, but I'm not in the mood for chitchat today."

His face fell, but he nodded as he stopped a few feet off from the counter. "Trouble with the missus, then?" He took my silence as agreement and glanced around the shop. "I'm sure a few sales'll get your spirits back up. Why're you still closed? It's peak hours."

"My little girl disappeared, Lionel," I said, unintentionally in almost a whisper. His mouth fell open in shock. "She went missing yesterday. No one's seen her since. Clara and I have looked everywhere. I'm afraid... I'm afraid someone's taken her."

"Aw, jeez, I'm sorry... That's awful." He looked regretful he'd even approached me. "I'm sure she's fine. It's not like she coulda gone far. I'm sure they'll find her soon."

"The police won't even start looking until tomorrow."

He sifted air through his teeth and lent a sympathetic nod. "That's capitalism for ya."

Not the words I wanted to hear. They almost made it sound like I'd asked for this.

"Does this kind of thing happen a lot down here?" I asked him. "Kids going missing?" I'd heard of it every now and then over the past three years, but nothing ever came of it. I always assumed the cases were resolved. That the children found their way home.

Lionel could only offer a shrug. "I guess ya hear about it from time to time, but that's no different from on the surface, right?"

"Was anyone ever caught? Did they ever identify any suspects?"

"I wouldn't know about details like that."

That I knew, but I had to ask anyway. Just to be sure.

"So you're convinced she didn't just run away on her own? Kids do that, ya know."

"Not Maddie."

He nodded solemnly. "I know it's not my place to say seeing as I only met her a couple of times, but I have to say I agree with ya on that. She certainly doesn't seem the type." He braced his elbow against the counter, dipping his head lower. "If you're really thinkin' something nefarious might've happened, then perhaps there's a certain gentleman you should pay a visit to," he said quietly, as if afraid of others overhearing, even though we were the only two in the shop.

"Who? You know people like that?"

"Wait, wait. Now I don't know him personally, but certainly three-quarters of Rapture knows *of* him," he said quickly, standing straighter. "Name is Peach Wilkins. Let's just say he makes his living doin' things that would make Andrew Ryan's head spin. But my point is this: this man Wilkins has got a reputation, you see? One for havin' things he got no business havin'. Just the other day I saw him smokin' down at Fighting McDonagh's. Smokin' *real* tobacco. So I wondered, where'd he get his grubby little hands on that? Rapture ain't seen the likes of real tobacco since... ever. Never were able to figure out how to make that stuff grow without soil." His wandering gaze returned to me. "Now I'm not sayin' he had no part in anything. But he certainly knows what's goin' on in the shadier side of Rapture."

Before I had a chance to think over everything he'd said, the phone rang. With lightning fast reflexes, I reached over my counter and snatched the receiver off the cradle, immediately bringing it up to my mouth.

"Hello? Maddie?" was my breathless greeting.

There was silence on the other end, and then Clara's voice.

"It's just me, Arthur," she said, her words trembling. "You've been gone so long. I had a feeling you were at the shop."

"It's not open. I'm just... I needed somewhere to think."

"I understand."

I waited a moment. She didn't continue. "What's wrong?" I glanced at Lionel. He gave an understanding nod and headed towards the door. "Did -- Has Maddie... ?"

"No, there's still no sign of her," she said, her voice barely above a whisper. "I just got a call from the police department. They said they won't be able to dispatch officers until tomorrow night."

"Why? But we paid them!"

"I know. I guess, something else has come up. That's what they said, at least. They're being paid two or three times that to investigate something else tonight. The whole department was practically rented out. They said there's nothing they can do about it. It's just... business."

"Like hell there's nothing they can do! What could possibly be more important than a missing child?"

"I asked. They wouldn't say."

My blood boiled at the thought. This dream of mine -- this free market wonderland -- was becoming my own personal hell. "Have you talked with the school yet? What'd they have to say?"

"Not much. They said if Maddie doesn't return by the end of the week, they'll be giving her spot to another child," she said, her voice breaking. "I've been talking with her friends and the other mothers.

31

No one's seen her or heard from her at all. The other girls couldn't think of any places she might've gone."

"I haven't had any luck, either," I said. "I feel like I've looked everywhere. Twice. No one's seen anything."

"Where could be possibly be? I'm starting to fear the worst, Arthur."

"No, honey, don't. We'll find her. I promise we'll find her, safe and sound. I'm not coming home until she's found. Don't worry about what the cops are doing. I'll find her myself."

***

Fish for Fortune at Neptune's Bounty read the plaque with a pelican and fish depicted on it in the terminal that led from the bathysphere station to what some called Port Neptune. Its official name was Neptune's Bounty.

It was where the bar known as Fighting McDonagh's was located, and hopefully, where I would get answers from this Peach Wilkins character.

Neptune's Bounty's docks and floor were busy with early-evening practices. Bringing in fishing subs and hauling out the day's catch. I wove my way through the massive complex labeled the Lower Wharf, on the lookout for McDonagh's sign.

Lionel had left without telling me what Peach looked like, so all I could do was go to the bar and ask around there. I wasn't sure what kind of place it was, but judging by the gruff and worn look of the dockworkers, I might stick out a little.

My presence went unnoticed or ignored for the most part as I found my way to a large set of stairs with a sign that read "To Upper Wharf." With no sign of the bar in sight, I took them. A red and white neon sign depicting a ship anchor told me I was in the right place. Below it was an open gate, beside which another bronze plaque hung, labeling the area as Pier 4. I stepped through the gate, past the stacks of cargo and length of thick rope that cluttered the floor.

Soon enough, the Fighting McDonagh's Tavern easily made itself known. It was the tallest building in the whole of Neptune's Bounty. A small staircase led up to its front door, which was dwarfed by the image of a large rooster-headed man with his hands raised, as if about to box. I could hear the shouts and cheers from inside before I even reached the door.

The tavern was packed, and as the door closed behind me, I found myself with little room to move. The interior was smaller than it looked, and much of that room was taken up by an actual boxing ring. Onlookers roared and whistled as two men went at it in the ring. Despite all the alcohol getting sloshed around with the ruckus, the place smelled like fish through and through.

Pushing through the crowd, passing by a set of shark jaws mounted on the wall, I made it to the surprisingly small bar, where several patrons -- including the bartender -- were also watching the fight. I took the lone empty stool and ordered a drink. This didn't look the kind of place where you could just waltz in and ask for info.

A scotch and two rounds in the ring later, the atmosphere changed. The two haggard men in the ring stepped down and talk was buzzing about the participants in the next match. Bets were placed. The bartender addressed me for the first time.

"Ain't never seen your face around here before. What brings ya?" he asked as he poured a beer for the gentleman sitting beside me.

I paused mid-sip. I couldn't stand waiting any longer, beating around the bush. "I'm looking for someone, actually. A gentleman by the name of Peach Wilkins. I hear he comes here." The last part was a lie. Lionel hadn't said anything about this being a frequent haunt of Peach's, but it was all I had to go on.

The bartender nodded, eyes closing slightly. He said something to the man next to me as he slid him his beer, and then his gaze turned to me. "Ya wanna see Peach, you say? And what business might you be wantin' with him?"

I shrugged, holding my near empty glass near my chin. "I've just got a few questions for him."

He nodded, snorting. "So Ryan's sending plainclothes in now, is he? That sure ain't his style."

Shit. "No, no," I said quickly. "I'm not a cop or anything like that."

"Right, right." The look he gave me was skeptical as he poured more drinks. "Even if you were, you'd be shit outta luck, messing with a guy like Peach." He laughed at the thought, then nodded his head towards an alcove at the side of the room. "You'll find your answers over there. The one who looks like he's taken a few too many punches."

I'd overlooked the alcove at first, but now, from this angle, I could see that it was more of a hallway. Probably led to a more private area.

"Thanks." I finished off my drink and counted out my bill, plus an extra ten. That was almost all I had on me at the moment. The rest had gone to covering those few spare dollars we couldn't scrape up for Poppadopolis.

"Come again," the bartender said with a grin as he scooped up the money and empty glass. He started to whistle as I left the counter and made my way across the room.

Another match had started, and the raucous atmosphere had returned.

Sure enough, the little offshoot led to a private room. The diamond wallpaper was alternating shades of beige and baby food green. A small card table was set up in the back of the room. Three men sat at it. And they all noticed me at the very same moment. Three sets of eyes boring into me like I'd just stepped into a lion's den.

It was impossible to tell which one was Peach. They all looked pretty rough. The one sitting on the right side of the table stood quickly, knocking the chips and cards all across the felt surface.

"Take a wrong turn, did you?" he asked, wiping his nose.

"Lookit what you did, Sammy, now all the chips and shit are mixed up," the man on the left said, scowling as he threw down the two cards he was holding. "And I had a fucking good hand, too!"

"What do you want, you dandy?" the third man sitting at the table's center asked, staring at me with steely cold eyes. He cocked his head to the side, and the lone overhead light highlighted the bend in his nose. His face looked worn. Deep creases ran from his nose to his mouth, and his wispy hair shot off in tufts over his half-bald head.

"I'm here to talk to Peach Wilkins," I replied. "I'm not a cop or anything. I'm just trying to get some answers about something, and I heard Peach might know."

"Yeah? And why's that?" the man with the crooked nose asked.

The standing man spat. "You really think you can just waltz in here with your fancy clothes and -- "

"It's my kid. My kid's gone missing, and I heard you might know something about it. Or about the other times it's happened, at least," I said quickly, wary of the man on the right as he neared.

"Stand down, Sammy G. Ol' Peach has got a customer, it looks like," the man with the bent nose said. Peach said. "How about you and Tommy go get me another beer while I talk to this gentleman?"

It wasn't a question. The men flanking him immediately hopped to it, brushing past me, one of them knocking into my shoulder. Once they were gone, Peach indicated the seat to his right.

"You got two minutes 'til they come back, and then I'm done listening." He gathered up the strewn cards and started shuffling them. "You say your little girl went missing? How old? Six or seven, I'm guessing."

"How did you know?"

"It's a story I've heard before, kid. A story everyone's heard before."

"I've lived here three years and I never heard anything about it," I said, confused.

"That's 'cause you live on the wrong side of Rapture. Or the right side, rather. Usually this sorta thing happens to people... of a lower class," he explained, tossing the deck of cards onto the table. "Now you mind telling me why in the hell you think I got anything to do with this? Do I look like the 'napping type?"

"That's not it. I was told you might have information. That's all."

"Yeah? Information about what? It's not like I know anything more than you do, kid. Little girls go missing down here every now and then. Been happening for a few years now. Cases never get solved. Even the papers know that much. Maybe you been reading the wrong papers."

"Only girls?"

He nodded. "Makes you wonder, doesn't it?"

I felt sick. "How could this be going on for so long?"

He gave a high-pitched laugh. More like a cackle. "You forgetting where we are, boy. This is Rapture. Ryan's playground. Built on freedom of everything. You really think he'd go out of his way to lock up some deviant when he ain't even cracking down on splicing? You say you've been here three years, but I don't believe it." He snorted in disgust as his two card buddies returned. "Looks like your time's up."

"Wait. Don't you know anything that -- "

"Didn't ya hear him? Boss says time's up," one of the men said as he grabbed me by the shoulder and knocked me from the chair. I stumbled but caught myself as he reeled back for a punch. Dodging his fist as it flew towards my face, my right hand made contact with the left side of his jaw. He stumbled back into the table.

The other man slammed the drinks onto the table. "You don't know who you're messing with, ya fucking dandy!"

"We got a game here to finish, Sammy G," Peach said, seemingly unperturbed by the commotion. I wiped off the blood that seeped through the cracked skin along my knuckles as the one I'd punched staggered to his feet. "You might want to pay a visit to Madame Fiona," Peach said as he looked at me, paying the man no mind. "She and her little crystal ball might be able to help you out."

I turned on my heel to leave.

"Wait," Peach called out.

I looked at him from over my shoulder.

"Now how about a little gratuity?" he said with a crooked grin.

Taking the last of the bills from my wallet, I tossed them towards him.

He watched with a smile as Sammy G rushed to collect them.

***

Madame Fiona's was a small sliver of a building wedged along the boardwalk of High Street. I'd never given it a second look, but I had heard her name before. Sometimes from Clara, when she was talking about her friends, but usually from the daily paper.

Madame Fiona ran a horoscope column in the Rapture Tribune. Rapture's Premier Fortune Teller she called herself. My guess is she was the only fortune teller.

Apparently it was a slow day, because once I dealt with the receptionist, I was ushered right up to Madame Fiona's room. It was everything I'd expected. Gypsy-like, with pillows and curtains everywhere in ugly shades. Noxious incense filled the air. A thin dark-skinned woman with black hair sat cross-legged on a pillow as she hunched over a literal crystal ball.

I was getting the feeling Peach had pulled my leg.

"You are here for an urgent matter," this woman -- Madame Fiona, I'm guessing -- said in a lilting voice, not looking up from her ball. The room was dark, but the ball seemed to be glowing as she circled her hands around it.

"Yeah, never mind." This was stupid.

"If you leave without asking, you leave without answers. And if you leave without answers, you'll never find her," she said just as I was heading back for the door.

I froze.

She smiled up at me.

"Have a seat, Mr. Winters," she said, gesturing to the pillow across from her. "And ask me your questions."

I kept my expression nonchalant but did as she bid anyway. "How do you know my name?"

"That's a rather boring question."

"Then how about this: How did you know I'm looking for someone?"

"News travels fast around Rapture," she said with a sigh, her voice dropping its sing-song quality. She picked up the crystal ball from its gilded pedestal and pressed a small button on its bottom. It promptly stopped glowing. She tossed it into the sea of pillows. "Let's just say that I make it my business to know what's going on down here at all times."

"You sure dropped the act quick."

She shrugged. "It's been my experience that parents with missing children don't like to be toyed with."

I didn't like the sound of this. "How much do you know?"

"I know that your daughter went missing yesterday," she said simply, propping her elbow against her knee and resting her chin against her hand. "A cute little thing. Seven, if I remember right. She attends the Ryan the Lion Prep Academy. Disappeared somewhere at Fontaine's Department Store, correct?"

I nodded. "I hear it's not the first time this kind of thing has happened. Other little girls have been kidnapped, too. Is that true? Where are they taken? I have to find -- "

"I'm an information broker, not a genie, Mr. Winters," she said tiredly as her eyes drifted over me. She held out her hand, palm up. "Your end first, of course."

Fuck, she wanted money.

"I don't have any," I admitted. The Fighting McDonagh's had cleaned me out.

40

Her brow knit. She sat back, crossing her arms over her bare midriff. "Well, isn't that lovely."

"But I can get you some in a few days," I said. Or rather, lied. At this rate, it'd be difficult to even pay this month's rents without cutting a few corners.

"I don't work on credit, Mr. Winters."

"But this is about my daughter. It's about a human *life*."

"Maybe to you. But to me, it's just business. It's just money," she said, sighing heavily. She sat back on her pillow and just stared at me, expectant.

As I reached for my wallet again, to make sure I hadn't missed any stray bills, something caught my eye. The glint of silver at my wrist. A watch I'd had for over ten years. The only thing the old man back in Cleveland had left me. Solid silver band and sapphires and diamonds in the face. A custom order no one had ever come to pick up. Too expensive to find a buyer for it at the time.

Without a second thought, I unclasped it from my wrist and handed it to her. She gave me a skeptical look -- perhaps at the blood that crusted my knuckles -- before taking it.

"Will that cover it?" I asked. "It's worth at least a grand, easy. Not to mention it's from the surface."

"The surface, you say," she repeated, one eyebrow quirking as she briefly glanced at me. Her thumb brushed over its face. She checked the back, inspected the links. "I suppose it'll do." She dropped it into her shirt, between her breasts, and sat forward, hands on her knees. "There's somewhere you need to go. Rather, some*one* you need to go to. I have a feeling he'll have all the answers to your questions, but it won't be easy."

I frowned. "Why's that? Who is he?"

She shook her head quickly, effectively pushing all my questions aside. "How about this? You'll escort my good friend to the Nyx Room tonight." She stood up and added, looking down on me, "Without her, you'll never get in. Once you're there, it's up to you to find the answers for yourself."

"Wait. Who am I supposed to meet? Why can't you just tell me? That watch is worth a hell of a lot more than information that vague."

"The watch is for renting Kirsi for the evening," she said simply. "She doesn't come cheap, you know."

***

"You must be Arthur Winters," an unfamiliar voice said.

My attention slid from the trail of smoke rising from the end of my cigarette to the blonde woman who stood before me. She wore a tight blue dress. A fur coat was folded and draped over her right arm.

It was about fucking time. I'd been standing here outside Worley Winery, waiting for this Kirsi girl for nearly a half hour.

"Yeah, that's me." I took a last puff and then put out my cig on the bottom of my shoe. "Fiona said you could help me."

"Mm. Maybe. But think of it more like you can help yourself," she said, her voice thick with a Scandinavian accent. She pulled on her jacket and fluffed her hair. "Let us be going now," she said as she began to walk down the street, her high heels clicking. "Otherwise, you might miss your opportunity."

I caught up with her, my irritation growing. Why wouldn't anyone just tell me what the hell was going on? All I wanted was to find Maddie. It was almost like folks were getting shits and giggles out of yanking me around.

"Why do I need to meet this guy?" I asked as we walked. I didn't know where the Nyx Room was, though I'd heard of it. I counted on her to lead the way. "Is he going to tell me where my daughter is, or is he just going to send me to someone else?"

"Oh, Clifford will not be telling you anything," Kirsi said with a short laugh. "He will be telling *me*, and you will be along for ride."

"What the hell is that supposed to mean?"

"It simple, really," she said, sliding her hands into the pockets of her coat. "He is assistant to Dr. Suchong. You know his name, yes?" She glanced at me for confirmation. I nodded, though I'd only heard the man's name in passing once or twice. He was a scientist of some sort. "My dear friend Fiona says he will have answers for you, so I'm sure answers he will have. Though what they are, I do not know either. She told me very little this time."

Well, that answered my question. But it made a little more sense. Kirsi was an escort, and she made rich, high-ranking drunk men spill their secrets. Then she provided Fiona with the info.

"Your eyes say you have more question," Kirsi said, frowning up at me.

43

I shook my head. "No, I'm just worried."

"You need not," she replied quickly. "No one will find you out of place if you stay at my side."

"That's not what I mean. I mean my daughter. I just want to find her." Every minute that had passed since she'd disappeared felt like wasted time. I wouldn't be able to bear it if it turned out I was too late.

"Well, you will need patience," she said matter-of-factly, as if it was the most obvious thing.

"You clearly don't have any kids."

She merely scoffed in response.

After leading me on a fifteen-minute walk that seemingly spanned the entire length of Rapture, we arrived at Fort Frolic. A place I'd only ever visited for the casino, and Clara, for the clothing store. Occasionally we hit the restaurants or theatre, but I'd never actually explored the whole area.

It was late evening, and the atrium was packed. Kirsi pointed with one heavily-lacquered fingernail up at the second floor of stores. There it was. A black and purple neon sign that read: *The Nyx Room*.

As we went up the stairs leading to it, Kirsi linked her arm around mine. My instinct was to escape her grip, but her hand tightened on my arm.

"And try to smile," she told me. "You have pretty girl on arm. People will wonder if you're not enjoying yourself."

I didn't smile, but I didn't try removing my arm again, either. I'd apologize to Clara later.

At the door, we were greeted by a large man who stood guard, a cigar hanging off his lip.

"Good to see you again, Chester," Kirsi purred as he turned to open the door.

His eye twitched as he looked at me. "Eh. Who's the stiff?"

"My new best friend, of course," she said with a giggle, leading me past him and into the club.

Chester merely grunted in return.

The room was large and dark. The walls and ceiling were a deep violet. The carpet was black. The lights were few and far between, and most were concentrated on a stage where a woman was dancing in nothing but her undergarments. Kirsi yanked me through the crowd, unafraid to elbow people of obstruction out of the way.

A slow, heavy beat accompanied with brass and strings filled the room. It was so loud it felt like the very ground was beating along with it.

Kirsi brought us to the bar, which was mostly empty. She let go of my arm long enough to lean over the counter and give the bartender a peck on the cheek.

"Hello, Donald. Is Clifford here yet?" she asked with a sweet smile.

The balding man nodded. "Same room as always, baby doll."

"Thank you very much." Kirsi snagged her arm around mine again and made a beeline for a hallway at the back of the room that had been hidden from afar. It was narrow, with only floor lights to guide the way. "He always drink in private room, because even he has a little brain," Kirsi explained as we walked. "He know he may leak secret."

45

The closed door she brought us to had no marker on it. She knocked four times and called out to Clifford in a breathy voice.

A moment later, the door opened. It was a woman -- one almost as beautiful as Kirsi. She immediately stepped aside, and Kirsi strode in, dragging me with her.

The room was small. Only big enough for two couches and a coffee table sandwiched between them. One was a two-seater, but the other was a large u-shape that could've seated seven or eight.

On that couch was a pudgy man with a head of wild, frizzy blond hair. He slouched with his arms hooked over the back of the couch as he twisted his neck to see Kirsi.

"Kirsi! Well I'll be damned. You said you didn't work Thursdays." A grin spread across his face as the other woman sat down next to him. He promptly shooed her away and then looked to me. "You mind a trade? Kirsi's kind of my girl."

"That will be fine," Kirsi said quickly, taking the spot the other woman had left when she stood. "This fellow does not much like me anyway." She snuggled into him as she spoke, and glanced up at me through thick lashes. "Don't be shy. Have your fun with Lydia."

"No thanks," I said, offering an apologetic smile to Lydia. That's not what I came here for. I came for answers.

"What's this?" Kirsi said, raising the only open wine bottle on the table. She sloshed it around. "The bottle still half-full. This isn't like you, Clifford. Let us fix that." She sat forward and started pouring two glasses of wine.

Lydia grabbed my hand and pulled me down onto the sofa with her. She was brunette and green-eyed, with her hair in a long bob Clara had recently contemplated getting.

"And what is your name?" she asked, her voice air thin. "I don't think I've seen you around here before."

"My name is Arthur."

"Hm?" She raised one thin eyebrow expectantly as she traced her finger along my sleeve. "Is that it? You won't tell me your last name?"

"Not tonight." Not ever.

She giggled. "Well, that's okay."

We made small talk for about ten minutes. My patience was wearing thin. Kirsi was still on the couch with this Clifford fellow, pouring drinks into him as he babbled. Lydia kept crowding close as I pretended to listen to whatever she was saying.

When she started to knead my thigh with her fingers, I moved her hand away. That's when I noticed a series of small red dots clustered near the inside of her elbow. Half a dozen tiny scabs, a few edged with yellowish purple bruises.

"What happened there?" I asked.

She glanced where I was looking and laughed. "Nothing *happened*, silly," she said, tucking her arm away at her side. "It's just from my ADAM shots."

I felt like I'd heard the phrase used before, but I couldn't place it. "ADAM shots?"

"Our lovely Lydia here has Plasmid, you see," Kirsi spoke up from where she sat on Clifford's lap. "Go ahead," she urged. "Show Arthur."

Lydia smiled and raised her hand. She spread it wide, fingers tensing. I wasn't sure what to expect.

And then a wine bottle from the table shot right into her palm. She closed her hand over it and grinned at me. "This one's Telekinesis. Isn't that amazing? Don't tell me you've never seen it before."

"Can't say I have," I said, giving a nervous laugh. ADAM. The life-force behind Plasmids -- the superhuman abilities scientists in Rapture alone had managed to create. "I've seen the ads, but..."

"Not everyone can afford it. And those who can like to keep their Plasmids hidden, usually. Even this far under the ocean, people will still find reasons to hate."

I watched as she sent the bottle back to the table using Telekinesis. "Isn't it a drug?"

"Yes, but it is not like those street drugs you find on surface," Kirsi said as she traced circles on Clifford's chest with her long fingernails. "Isn't that right, Clifford? You would know better than I or Lydia." Her eyes drifted to me, a smirk twisting her lips.

"Well, we really don't know enough about ADAM or Plasmids yet, to be perfectly honest," Clifford replied, slurring his words, but perfectly coherent. "We've only been down here ten years. It won't be another twenty, thirty years before we know the real risks and long-term effects of either..."

This was all interesting, but I didn't care.

"But that doesn't stop people from getting hooked right quick," he continued, pushing Kirsi aside as he leaned forward for another bottle of wine. His clumsy hands fumbled with the corkscrew and Kirsi rolled her eyes as she grabbed both from him. "At the rate we were going for a while, an ADAM shortage was a sure thing. We've looked all over the goddamn ocean, but the only organism that can produce the stuff is a sea slug. Can you believe that? An entire drug industry reliant on a fat slimy worm. And even the slug's output is abysmal. Thank God for Little Sisters, or I'd be out a job..."

"Little Sisters?" I asked, frowning. The only time I'd heard the term was in relation to Frank Fontaine's Little Sister's Orphanage.

"Ugh..." The man belched and grimaced. "I shouldn't really be talking about this, you know."

Kirsi rested her head against his shoulder. "Go on, Clifford. I am also curious about these Little Sisters."

"Well, it's pretty simple, really," he continued, easily convinced. "We at Dr. Suchong's lab spent a hell of a lot of time trying to figure out ways to produce ADAM faster and more efficiently. But humans are a veritable goldmine -- little girls to be specific." Kirsi poured him a glass and he took a sip. "We implanted the sea slug in an array of subjects, but it was only in the stomach of little girls that we found real results. ADAM production was increased twenty, thirty percent. It was nothing short of amazing."

Lydia settled against my shoulder. "Why only girls, I wonder?"

Clifford shrugged. "We've never been able to figure that out, either. But we've run all sorts of tests. Little boys are no good. Even adolescent girls are too old. It's a very specific window of time, and a peculiar one at that."

I didn't like what I was hearing. "Where do they get the little girls for this?"

"From The Little Sister's Orphanage, of course," he said, as if I was stupid for not knowing. "Hence the name. Oh, don't me give that look. If it wasn't for the demand for ADAM, those girls would've just been cast off into the street and died like dogs. The orphanage takes good care of them, I'll have you know.

"Although, the recent ADAM boom, facilitated by our creation of the Little Sisters, has brought us a rather ironic problem. We're running short on ADAM again. Apparently there aren't enough unwanted little girls in the world. Or Rapture, at least. So lately we've been resorting to *other* methods to procure more hosts."

Suddenly, it all made sense. Why Fiona had sent me here, and why Kirsi wanted me to meet Clifford. I stood up slowly, my fists clenching. "And by hosts, you mean little girls."

He scowled at me. "Of course. Haven't you been listening?"

"How many of these orphanages are there?"

"Two. One in Hestia Chambers, and one in Plaza Hedone," Lydia spoke up, looking perturbed. "But Arthur -- "

The rest of her sentence fell of deaf ears as I dashed out of the room and down the hall. I bowled my way through the crowd in the dark and quickly found the door.

Plaza Hedone was an apartment complex in Siren Alley -- essentially the red light district of Rapture. It was located somewhere between Dionysus Park and Pauper's Drop. Hestia Chambers, I was more familiar with. It was in Apollo Square, after all. Where we'd lived for three years before making the move to Olympus Heights.

I headed for Hestia first, my heart leaping into my throat all the while. The train took me there quickly, and I pushed through the mob of people waiting to board at the station like a madman. Some shoved back, others yelled. I ignored them altogether and raced towards Apollo Square.

The place was just as humble and unfortunate as when I'd left it. Perhaps even more so, now. I ran past Artemis Suites and the bathysphere port before finally arriving at Hestia Chambers' doorstep. It was a large building of half a dozen floors.

The lobby doors opened easily. Inside, there were various double doors and signs that hung over them. One advertised Fontaine's Center for the Poor. Another was Fontaine's Little Sister's Orphanage.

I entered the orphanage, slowing my pace. If Maddie was here, if I could catch her alone, I could just grab her and run. The front desk I passed was empty, but there were sounds coming from further down the hallway. The voices of young girls as they laughed and sang and played.

"Maddie?" I couldn't help myself. I could've sworn I heard her voice amongst them. I sprinted down the hall and turned into the area it led into. A handful of little girls dotted the room. Several sat on the floor, several on bunk beds. One stood idly in the doorway to another room.

They all stared back at me, their laughter and chatter ceasing. My eyes quickly swept over each of them. They all looked the same age -- between six and eight. Clifford hadn't been lying. My heart sank.

They all wore soiled dresses and were barefoot.

But none of them were Maddie.

I turned to the one standing closest to me. She shirked away as I grabbed her shoulders. "Is there a girl here named Maddie?" I asked her feverishly.

There was a look of fear on her face as she shook her head and squirmed.

I let go and directed my attention to the others. "Does anyone know of a girl named Maddie here? She's seven. Red hair, blue eyes."

They all merely backed away, shaking their heads collectively.

"Excuse me, sir," a voice from behind me said. I whirled around to see a tall woman staring me down. Her hands propped against her hips. "Just what do you think you're doing here?"

"I'm looking for my daughter. Maddie. She went missing yesterday," I said quickly, the words coming out in a rush. "I think she might be here. Do you know her?"

"Sir, it is not in our policy to return orphans after they've been given up."

"I didn't give her up! She was taken. Someone *stole* her." Realizing I wasn't going to get anywhere with this woman, I stumbled past the girls and into the next room. The woman shouted after me as I explored from room to room, looking for Maddie. Calling for her. There were other little girls. All in the same sad state as the ones in the first room. By the time I came to the last room, I had to accept the fact that my little girl was not among them.

As I gripped tightly one of the rickety metal posts of a bunk bed in one of the crowded rooms, the woman caught up to me. She stopped in the doorway of the bedroom just as I looked up.

"Your child has been chosen for a role far more important than that of a mere daughter," she said as she extended her arm towards me. "You should be proud."

Her hand glowed blow and before I knew what was happening, a bolt of electricity shot out of her palm. Immediately, I was engulfed.

In the next moment, the world went black.

***

I opened my eyes to an unfamiliar ceiling. My vision was fuzzy.

"Finally comin' around, huh? I was worried you were a goner," someone said with a laugh. It was a voice I recognized. Lionel Groose.

As I sat up, he plopped down onto a chair next to the bed I was on. How the hell...? Where were we, even? I looked around, but came up empty. I felt like my body was buzzing, as if it were numb, but not really.

"Whoa, there, pal. You shouldn't be gettin' up or anything just yet."

"Why?" I asked. Why did I feel like shit? And why couldn't I remember how I'd gotten here?"

"Well, from the looks of ya, someone used to Electro Bolt on you," Lionel replied, handing a mug of water to me.

I reached for it, then winced as sharp pains shot through my hand. That's when I realized it was wrapped with a bandage. The other one, too.

And then I remembered. The woman at the Little Sister's Orphanage. The electric shock.

"So I'm walking home through Apollo Square and what do I see lying on the street in front of Hestia Chambers? Good old Arthur Winters heaped up in a pile. Thought you were dead, but you had a pulse, so I dragged you back here and tried to keep it that way." He looked pleased with himself as I gingerly took the cup and drank. "Did a pretty good job of it, too, if I don't say so myself."

"Thanks," I managed, cringing. It wasn't just my hands that hurt. My whole body did. My skin itself felt tender, like a terrible sunburn.

"I would've taken you down to the Medical Pavilion, but even an IV drip there costs a fortune, and you know I've been a little down in my luck lately..." He trailed off, running a hand through his disheveled hair. "Anyway, what the hell were you doing down there? This doesn't have anything to do with your daughter, does it?"

At that, I could only nod. He looked mortified.

"Oh, God, I'm sorry, man. I thought for sure she'd be back by now."

"So did I. Or so I hoped." When I moved to set down the coffee cup, he sprang up from the chair and took it for me. "Where are we? Is this your place?"

"Yeah! Sure thing," he said, his mood brightening as he placed the cup on the bedside table. "I couldn't remember your apartment number over at Olympus Heights, and this was a much shorter trip."

"Thanks again, Lionel. I mean it."

"No problem. What're friends for, after all," he said with a grin and a chuckle. "So, exactly what was it you were doing there, anyway? Looking for leads?"

"No. Looking for Maddie. I heard she might be at that Fontaine's Little Sister's Orphanage," I replied, earning a surprised look from him.

"You think she's at one of those orphanages? What the hell made you think that?"

I'd expected that kind of reaction. "It's a long story. I'll tell you about it later, once I get her back."

"And... so? Was she there?" he asked warily.

I shook my head. "I searched the place top to bottom, but she wasn't. There were a lot of other girls like her, though."

"Girls like her?"

"There's another place I have to look. There's another one of those orphanages over in Siren Alley. It's at Plaza Hedone."

"Don't tell me you're thinking of heading over there next."

"Of course I am."

Lionel rubbed the stubble on his chin, eyes narrowed as if in deep thought. "So it sounds like you're sayin' Fontaine's up to something shady at these orphanages."

"That's about it." I slowly sat up, cringing at the pain the simple movement caused. My vision still wasn't entirely clear, and my fingers felt like they were vibrating. But I was glad just to be alive. "Anyway, I have to get to -- "

"Buddy, you're not gonna just waltz up to the other orphanage in Siren Alley and find your little girl, if that's what you think," he said. "Chances are Fontaine's already heard of your little incident at Hestia Chambers. He'll have people on the lookout for ya."

"Then what the hell am I supposed to do?" I nearly shouted. "If there's any chance that Maddie's there... I have to find her."

"You will. You will, believe me." He gave a few quick nods, as if reassuring himself. "And you know why? 'Cause Lionel Groose just happens to work at Bathysphere DeLuxe, and he got access to a bathysphere. If we take that instead of using the trains, we can sneak up to the back entrances of Siren Alley and they won't even see us coming."

***

"I can't believe you can get your hands on a private bathysphere like this," I said, standing close to the bubble of glass, watching Rapture glide by.

"Well, to be fair, it's not really mine," he said from where he slouched against the curved wall. "I'm supposed to be fixin' it for a customer, but a little excursion like this won't do this baby no harm."

"How long until we get there?"

56

"About another fifteen minutes, I'd say. This thing's a little old, so she don't move as fast as the rest."

I was glad she moved at all. If it wasn't for Lionel, getting to Plaza Hedone would either be immensely difficult or altogether impossible.

I spent the next ten minutes trying to come up with a plan. Once I was in Plaza Hedone, exactly how would I go about getting Maddie? If there were more people with those Plasmids, I was a goner for sure.

I was still contemplating it when I noticed something odd. The buildings we were passing -- this was the more industrial part of Rapture, somewhere nestled between Dionysus Park and Outer Persephone.

In other words, we'd already passed Siren Alley.

Just as I realized it, a large building came into view. A tall monolith labeled Fontaine Futuristics.

When I turned to look at Lionel, he stiffened.

"What is this?" I asked, snatching him by the collar.

"What is what? It's business, of course," he said, letting out a shaky laugh. "This is Rapture, Arthur. Everything's about money down here."

"What the hell is that supposed to mean?"

"It means if Fontaine wants to pay me a little somethin' extra and give me my own bathysphere just for 'napping a few kids for his little abomination program, then why not?"

I slugged him across the face, sending him into the wall. His hands came over his face as blood started to pour from his nose. But despite that, he was laughing.

"Welcome to Rapture, pal."

Before I could wind back for another punch, he thrust his hand out to me, fingers splayed. A blast of ice hit me. Every inch of me was frozen. My already blurry grew worse. I couldn't move a muscle. The darkness crept in again.

The last words I heard were, "Peach was supposed to kill ya, you know. Fickle bastard..."

***

My throat hurts...

It was all I could think. As I regained consciousness, it was the only thing that truly registered in my mind. Before even opening my eyes, I reached up to feel my throat. To figure out why it hurt.

But where fingers should have met neck, I felt something else. My arm was heavy, and clad in thick gloves. When my fingers brushed against my throat, all I felt was metal.

I opened my eyes and felt like a fish inside a bowl. A pane of rounded glass obstructed a clear view of what was before me.

I looked down. The movement was difficult. I was wearing a heavy diving suit. Instead of a hand, a large drill hung from the end of my right arm.

Am I a diver? I couldn't even remember who I was, let alone *what* I was, or how I'd got here. Wherever here was.

Across the room, past a wall of glass, a woman knelt next to a little girl. They were speaking. I had to strain to hear over the sound of my own labored breathing.

" -- and Mr. Bubbles will protect you no matter what, okay?" the woman said. "So get out there and collect as much as you can. Got it?"

The girl gave a fervent nod, her ponytail shaking. The woman stood up and said something else too low for me to hear. The girl then skipped out of sight, and the woman left, too. I stared at the empty room until the door opened on this side.

It was the girl, red haired. She wore a tattered green dress. Her eyes glowed yellow from darkened sockets.

She looked up at me and smiled.

"Mr. Bubbles!" she cried, running over to me. "You're awake, Mr. Bubbles! You took such a long nappy nap." She took my hand and began leading me out of the room. "Let's go, Mr. B! Let's go to where the angels are!"

I haltingly followed, plodding along behind her.

She seemed familiar, somehow.

Skipping along, she hummed, her red ponytail switching back and forth.

I watched it, mesmerized.

Then suddenly, a name came to me. I don't know from where, but it felt right.

"Maddie?" I said.

But the only sound that left my throat was a mournful growl.

Thank you for reading

Thank you for reading my book. I hope you enjoyed it. If you did I would really appreciate it if you left me a review.

Ratings and reviews are **extremely helpful** and greatly appreciated! They do matter in the rankings of the book, and I read each and every one of them.

Also if you would like to be notified when my new books are free on Kindle and get exclusive short stories delivered directly to your inbox.
Please sign up here -
http://www.dustinbrubaker.com/

87696217R00035

Made in the USA
San Bernardino, CA
06 September 2018